WARTON
AND THE
CONTEST

WARTON
AND THE
CONTEST
BY RUSSELL E. ERICKSON

PICTURES BY LAWRENCE DI FIORI

LOTHROP, LEE & SHEPARD BOOKS
NEW YORK

Library of Congress Cataloging in Publication Data
Erickson, Russell E. Warton and the contest.

Summary: When the crow steals Grampa Arbuckle's watch-compass, the two toad brothers, Warton and Morton, try to get it back with the help of an accident-prone mouse and a blind blue jay.

[1. Toads—Fiction. 2. Mice—Fiction. 3. Birds—Fiction. 4. Friendship—Fiction] I. Di Fiori, Lawrence, ill. II. Title.

PZ7.E7257Warf 1986   [E]   86-102
ISBN 0-688-05818-3
ISBN 0-688-05819-1 (lib. bdg.)

Also by Russell E. Erickson

A Toad For Tuesday
Warton and Morton
Warton's Christmas Eve Adventure
Warton and the King of the Skies
Warton and the Traders
Warton and the Castaways

The dark of night had long been upon the deep forest. It now lay in near perfect stillness. Winds were calm, birds were silent, and most creatures, except those that prowl with stealthy feet and glowing eyes, were asleep.

Or they were preparing for sleep. That is what the toad brothers, Warton and Morton, were doing down in their snug home. Sitting at the kitchen table, where dominoes were scattered all about, they watched as Grampa Arbuckle, who lived next door, pulled out his favorite possession—a gold combination watch-compass.

"Hmmmph," said the old toad. "That will be enough for one evening. Look." He placed the watch-compass on the table.

"It's way past our bedtime," said Morton.

Warton was shaking his head. "And neither of us has won a game yet."

Grampa Arbuckle chuckled. "Don't feel too bad. It's not easy to beat a domino champion—someone who has played in tournaments throughout the forest, someone who even beat the frogs last year to win this beautiful watch-compass." He narrowed his eyes. "And you know how frogs cheat."

Warton and Morton nodded.

Then Grampa Arbuckle said good night. He went into the parlor, where he entered a passageway that connected the two homes. When he was gone, Warton began gathering up the dominoes while Morton put away cups and saucers.

"Oh-oh," said Warton. "Grampa Arbuckle left his watch-compass on the table."

"We'd better take it to him right away," said Morton. "You know how he treasures it."

"I do," said Warton. "But he may be asleep already. I'll take it to him in the morning."

"Well then, I'm off to bed myself," said Morton. "I've a busy day of cooking ahead of me."

"And I've lots of cleaning to do," said Warton, yawning.

The two toads were soon in their beds, where they

drifted off to sleep on soft cattail-stuffed mattresses. For the rest of the night, except for the ticking of the mantel clock, all was quiet. Then, just before dawn, there came the sound of breaking glass.

Warton's eyes popped open. "Morton, was that you?" he called.

"No," answered a sleepy voice from the next room. "It came from the cellar."

Warton quickly hopped out of bed. Dressed in red-and-white-striped pajamas, he lit a candle and went into the kitchen, where Morton, wrapped in a woolly bathrobe and holding a sturdy potato masher, waited. Warton opened a wooden door in the pantry, and stealthily the two toads went down narrow stairs to the cellar. They peered into each dark corner.

Morton cried out suddenly. He pointed to where several broken jars lay in a purple puddle on the floor. "My elderberry jelly! Every jar is smashed!"

Warton studied the mess closely. "Whoever did this has left footprints of jelly. I'm going to follow them."

Holding the candle close to the floor, he followed the tracks around an old chair and a dusty table, between flour barrels and boxes of salt, behind a dresser to a wardrobe closet. Then he stopped. The footprints went no farther. Warton walked around the wardrobe twice. He put his eye to the keyhole. At once, a startled look came over his face and he jumped backward.

"Morton!" he cried. "I saw an eye looking back at me!"

"Oh no," said Morton. "Now what will we do?"

"I think we should capture whoever is in there," said Warton.

"I was afraid of that," said Morton.

Warton found a piece of rope and turned to his brother. "Is your potato masher ready?"

Morton nodded. Then the two toads took hold of the wardrobe and gave it a hard shove. It fell to the floor with a thud, and Warton flung open the door.

Sitting on the bottom of the closet, a dazed little creature looked up at the toads with dark round eyes.

"Why, it's a meadow mouse," said Warton.

"And there's no doubt it was he who was trying to steal my elderberry jelly," said Morton. "Look at him!"

Warton studied the little mouse. He saw a peaked cap with a visor, a green pullover shirt, brown shorts, and he saw one other thing. All over the mouse there were gobs of purple jelly.

Warton nodded. "There's no doubt about it, all right."

At that, the mouse's whiskers began twitching. "Is that so!" he cried. "Well, there happens to be plenty of doubt about it!"

"There is?" said the two toads together.

"Yes," said the mouse. "Finding broken jelly jars and me with jelly stains doesn't mean I was stealing from you."

"Then what *does* it mean?" said Morton.

"It means . . ." said the mouse, suddenly looking embarrassed, "it means it was an accident."

"An accident?" said Warton.

"Yes," said the mouse. "Earlier this evening, I came upon an old mole who was trying to catch a lizard. I decided to help him, and when the lizard went into a hole under a stump, I went in after him. I didn't know the stump was over your home, and somehow I came out right on top of your shelf of jelly jars, which fell to the floor. When I heard you coming, not knowing who lived here, I hid."

Warton could see the mouse was sincere. "I'm sorry I thought you were stealing jelly. I didn't realize it was an accident. That could happen to anyone."

"Not to anyone," said the mouse sadly. "You see, accidents are the reason I've left my home in the meadow where I lived with lots of other mice. Accidents have happened to me since the day I was born. Now no one even lets me come near, and when I go to visit, no one lets me in. So I've decided to go live someplace else."

Warton felt sorry for the little mouse. "Perhaps it only *seems* like you have more accidents than anyone else."

"Do you really think so?" said the mouse.

"It's very likely," said Warton. "In any case, you needn't leave the way you came in. You may use our kitchen door if you wish."

"And since I'm already up," said Morton, "I'm going to start breakfast. You're most welcome to have some."

The mouse looked delighted. "That's very nice of you," he said. "My name's Neville. What are yours?"

The toads told him their names. Then, as Neville climbed out of the wardrobe, their mouths dropped and they stared wide-eyed. Instead of a tail, Neville had a length of rope attached to a short stub.

The mouse noticed the toads' surprise. "Oh, I lost my real tail when I accidentally rocked over it in a rocking chair. After that I could walk only in circles. Then one day I thought of attaching the rope. It straightened me right out."

"A good idea," said Warton.

"Thank you," said Neville. "Now I think I should clean up the mess I caused." He started for a broom handle that was set under a shelf.

"Wait!" cried Morton.

It was too late. The broom handle, which had been holding up the shelf, came loose, and the shelf crashed to the floor.

"Oh no," moaned Morton. "My special jars of candied fruit flies. Now *they're* all broken!"

The mouse looked sadly at Morton. "I'm sorry," he said.

Morton swallowed hard. "Never mind. But I think we should all go upstairs as quickly as possible." He led the way to the kitchen, where he set right to work cooking.

Warton joined the mouse at the kitchen table. Wanting to cheer Neville up, he said, "It was nice of you to help that mole."

"Oh, I was glad to do it," said the mouse. "I like helping others. The trouble is, things never seem to go right." Then he brightened. "But I did help someone yesterday, and it turned out fine."

"What happened?" asked Warton.

"I helped a squirrel get rid of a poison ivy vine that grew around her tree. It was easy. All I had to do was build a fire around the bottom of the tree. In no time the vines were burning nicely, and I went on my way."

"How did you keep the tree from catching on fire too?" asked Warton.

Neville gave a start. "Oh, my. I hadn't thought of that. No wonder she was shouting as I walked off." He looked sad again.

Just then Morton came to the table. He set out a platter of smoked slug strips, three bowls of mealworm mush, and a tall stack of ryegrass toast.

Then the toads and the mouse ate breakfast.

"Mmm," said Neville after his second helping of everything. "That was tasty."

"I'm glad you liked it," said Morton, beaming.

"I did," said Neville as he stood up. "And to show my appreciation, I'm going to wash all the dirty dishes for you."

Morton looked horrified. "Oh no! You can't! I mean . . . you shouldn't bother!"

"It's no bother at all," said Neville. "Now you relax with your brother, and in a little while you won't know these dishes."

Morton whispered to Warton. "That's what I'm afraid of. They're going to end up like my preserve jars—in little pieces."

"Perhaps if we don't watch," said Warton, "things will go right for him."

"I'll try not to," said Morton.

Neville cleared the table quickly and filled the sink with dishes and bubbly water. Warton could see his brother waiting for the sound of breaking china, but no such sound came, and soon a stack of sparkling dishes stood on the counter.

Morton let out a long breath of air. "It looks like I was worried for nothing."

"It does," said Warton. "And that reminds me, I'd better return Grampa Arbuckle's watch-compass before *he* gets worried."

Warton looked about. "Morton, did you move it?"

"I left it exactly where it was," said Morton. "In the middle of the table."

"But it's not there," said Warton. "And if I didn't move it, and you didn't, where could it have gone?"

The two toads stared at each other. Then they turned to the sink just as Neville pulled a golden object out of the soapy water.

"The watch-compass!" they yelled, springing from their chairs.

Neville looked up. "Is that what this is?"

"It's our grandfather's most prized possession," said Warton.

"And now it's ruined," said Morton.

11

The mouse's face drooped. "I've done it again."

Warton could see how bad Neville felt. "Perhaps we can put it on the stove to dry."

Morton shook his head. "Too hot. A delicate instrument like this needs a gentle heat to dry it out."

"Do you mean like the sun on a flat rock?" said Neville.

Morton's eyes widened. "Why, yes. *That* just might work."

"Let's try it," said Warton.

"All right," said Morton. "I'll stay here in case Grampa Arbuckle comes by. We don't want him to worry."

Warton opened a door by the sink and led the way up a tunnel to the forest floor. There, he and Neville went to a flat rock warmed by the sun, and carefully they placed the watch-compass on it.

"Now we'll just have to wait," said Warton.

Although there were still a few small piles of snow around from the past winter, the early spring day was quite pleasant. Warton and Neville sat on a patch of moss. The moss was soft and the sunshine soothing. Soon Warton's eyes grew heavy. Finally he shut them, and he listened to the sounds of the forest—the caw of a crow, the buzz of a bee, the murmur of the pines.

When he heard the crow again he knew the bird must be close, for he heard the rustle of feathers. Then he heard the click of something touching metal. That sound made his eyes pop open. What he saw made him sit straight up. A large black crow was standing on the flat rock looking at the watch-compass with interest.

"Oh no!" cried Warton.

Warton and Neville rushed toward the crow, but before they were halfway there the bird rose from the rock. Clenched in his claws was the watch-compass. With a loud caw he disappeared over the trees.

Warton could say but one thing. "Poor Grampa Arbuckle."

Neville sighed. "If only I hadn't washed the dishes."

"If only I had taken the watch-compass to Grampa Arbuckle last night," said Warton.

Slowly they started back to the toads' home. At the bottom of the tunnel Warton heard Grampa Arbuckle's familiar voice beyond the door. With a feeling of dread he stepped inside.

"Hmmmph!" said the old toad, who was sitting at the kitchen table. "Here's Warton now, and he has a meadow mouse with him."

"This is Neville," said Warton. "He accidentally fell into our cellar last night."

"Accidents do happen," said Grampa Arbuckle.

"I know," said Neville. "That's how I happened to wash your watch-compass this morning."

Warton gulped. He hadn't expected the subject to be brought up so soon.

15

"So that's why everyone looks so forlorn," said Grampa Arbuckle. "Well, there's no need to worry any longer. That wonderful watch-compass is waterproof. That's why I love it so—there's not a thing that can happen to it."

Warton cleared his throat. "There is *one* thing," he said.

At that, Grampa Arbuckle appeared a bit unsettled. "What was that? What did you say?"

"Well," said Warton, who could not have felt worse, "a crow picked it up and flew off with it."

Grampa Arbuckle began to quiver. The quivering started at his toes and went all the way to his head. After a while he stopped, and he was perfectly still except for his cheeks, which puffed in and out. "Do you mean my watch-compass is gone?"

Warton nodded.

Morton quickly went into the pantry. No one spoke until he returned with a steaming pot. "This is licorice tea," he said. "It's the strongest tea there is—just what is needed at a time like this."

After a few sips everyone relaxed a bit.

"Hmmmph!" snorted Grampa Arbuckle. "I just

hope that crow realizes what a wonderful thing he has there. Perhaps crows don't know how to tell time or where the North Pole is." He looked about. "Does anyone know if crows are smart or dumb?"

When no one answered, Warton said, "I do know *one* thing. I've noticed that at this time of year they all fly in the same direction at dusk each day."

"And in the morning they come from the same direction," said Neville.

"That must mean," said Morton as he poured more tea, "that they have a certain place where they spend the night."

Grampa Arbuckle looked thoughtful. "Then it would seem to me that that place must be where my watch-compass is."

"And it seems to me," said Warton, "that if someone were to follow the crows, he'd find out where that place is."

"And it seems to me," said Neville, "that someone might even be able to get the watch-compass back."

Morton was shaking his head. "And it seems to me that even thinking of such things is ridiculous. That place where the crows go could be in a terrible part of the forest, and the crows—whom we know nothing about—could be even more terrible."

Grampa Arbuckle nodded. "Morton's right. The idea is ridiculous."

Warton and Neville nodded also.

Then Grampa Arbuckle got up. "I must be going now."

"It's time I was on my way, too," said Neville.

Everyone said good-bye, and when they were alone again, Warton said, "Morton, will you please make me enough sandwiches for a trip?"

"Certainly," said Morton, going to the bread box. He was opening the lid when a horrified look came over his face. "A trip!" he cried. He hurried back to his brother. "Warton, you don't intend to . . ."

"I do," said Warton. "I'm going to see if I can find the place where all the crows go each night."

"But, Warton . . ." said Morton. Then he stopped. He could tell by Warton's expression that his mind was made up. Letting out a big sigh, he returned to the bread box.

Warton went straight to his room. He quickly put on his broken-in walking boots, his heavy checkered

shirt, and his pants with the reinforced knee patches, and then he returned to the kitchen.

Morton was filling a pack with sandwiches. "I've made your favorite kinds," he said. "Cricket loaf and chopped aphid."

"Thank you," said Warton. "If I'm lucky, I'll be back soon."

"And if you're not lucky," said Morton solemnly, "you may not come back at all."

Warton slipped the filled pack on, and after fond good-byes he was on his way.

As soon as Warton stepped onto the forest floor he looked up at the sky. "Hmmm," he said, "not a crow in sight. But I know where the sun sets, so that's the direction I'll take."

Warton stepped out briskly. He loved going to new places. Softly, he hummed one tune after another as he passed under tall hemlocks, jumped over mossy logs, and circled crusty boulders.

It was noon when he came to a small meadow. After making sure there were no dangerous animals about, he started across. In the middle of the meadow he came to a lone tree—a spreading walnut. Its shade looked inviting, and he decided to have lunch there. He went to a flat rock surrounded by broken walnut shells, and after pushing two unopened walnuts off the rock, he sat down.

"Some squirrel must love living in this tree," he thought as he unwrapped a sandwich. Seeing a piece of walnut meat in one of the broken shells, he decided to taste it. He put his sandwich down and started toward the shell. Just as he did, a rock came crashing down out of the tree. Warton let out a yell, and when he looked at where he had been sitting, he saw his sandwich squashed flat.

Then a voice came from above him. "Is someone down there?"

"Yes," answered Warton. "And luckily I'm still alive." He looked up into the tree. On a limb far above he saw a blue jay.

"What kind of animal are you?" called the blue jay.

Warton blinked. "If you mean am I a frog or a toad, I'm a toad. My name is Warton."

The blue jay flew from the tree and landed near Warton. "My name is Bike," said the bird.

Warton wondered why the blue jay did not look directly at him, and instead cocked his head as if listening to something.

"Jump in the air, Warton," said the blue jay.

Warton was perplexed. Nevertheless he gave a small jump.

"That's the sound of a jumping toad, all right," said Bike.

All at once, Warton realized why the bird was not looking at him. "Why, you're blind," he said.

"I am," replied the blue jay. "So you can understand why I didn't know you were down here when I dropped the rock."

"I can," said Warton. "But why did you drop the rock?"

"It's the only way I have of opening walnuts," said Bike. "Although they're delicious, they have very hard shells."

Warton looked again at the rock. This time he noticed there was a vine wrapped around it. "That looks very heavy," he said.

"It's heavy, all right," said the blue jay. "And it took a lot of practice before I was strong enough to lift it. But now I can do it easily. Let me show you."

Warton watched as the blue jay took hold of the vine. As the bird began flapping his wings, Warton could see how powerful Bike was. Before long Bike was high in the air. Then he lit on a branch, moved a bit to one side, and let loose of the rock. It sped downward and smashed against the other rock just as before.

"You certainly are strong," said Warton when the

bird landed beside him. "But tell me, are walnuts the only thing you eat?"

"Not at all," said Bike. With that, the bird flew out over the meadow, and Warton watched as he darted this way and that, shot up and down, and made curves and loops. When he returned to Warton, he held a winged bug in his bill.

"I hear quite well," said the blue jay, "so I'm able to catch any bug that makes the slightest sound. I eat berries, too."

"But isn't doing all those things dangerous when you aren't able to see?" said Warton.

The bird shook his head. "I've learned the sounds of all the animals, and when I hear something suspicious, I fly into a hole in my tree. It's perfectly safe here for me. In fact, it's so safe here, it's monotonous."

"Monotonous?" said Warton.

"Oh yes," said the bird. "Sitting in a tree eating walnuts all day is not very exciting, you know. Why, last week I was so bored I decided to take a walk in the forest. I filled a large pack with string to help me find my way back, and off I went."

"What happened?" asked Warton.

24

"It was a very short walk," replied the blue jay. "After I bumped into nineteen trees and stumbled over twenty-seven rocks, I turned around and came home."

"I'm sorry it turned out that way," said Warton.

"So am I," said Bike. "Now tell me, what are you doing here?"

Warton took two sandwiches from his pack, and as he and the bird ate them he explained about Grampa Arbuckle's watch-compass.

Bike was fascinated by the story. "Where do you think the crows go?" he said when Warton finished.

"I don't know," replied Warton. "But if I'm ever to find out, I must be going." He stood up.

"Good-bye, Warton," said the bird. "If you pass this way again, please stop and say hello." He sighed. "I'm sure to be home."

"I will," promised Warton, and he was off.

When he reached the other side of the meadow, he entered a thicket of laurel bushes. The thick, twisted branches made the walking the worst he had ever seen. He was greatly relieved when at last he came to the end, and he stepped out to find himself at the top of a sandbank.

At the bottom of the sandbank he heard a commotion. There stood an angry chipmunk. She was shouting at someone lying in a heap with a basket of broken eggs on his head.

"Some help you are!" squeaked the chipmunk loudly.

A muffled voice came from under the basket. "But I was only trying to help. Falling down the sandbank was an accident." Then Neville the mouse sat up and held out the basket, which oozed stringy gobs of eggs.

"Just look at my basket!" squeaked the chipmunk. "My sister was expecting those eggs. Now what will I tell her?"

Neville looked at her sadly as egg yolk dripped from his ears. "You could say you already scrambled them for her."

At that, the chipmunk gave Neville an indignant look and snatched the basket from him. Then she spun around and hurried off.

Quickly, Warton hopped down the sandbank.

"Warton!" cried the mouse. "What are you doing here?"

"I'm searching for the place where the crows go."

"You are?" said Neville. "That's just what I'm doing. It's my fault the watch-compass is gone—because of my washing it—so I feel I should do whatever I can to get it back."

"That's very nice of you," said Warton. "But it's really my fault. I should have returned it the moment I discovered it."

For a few moments the toad and the mouse stared at each other. Then they broke into grins. "We'll go there together," they said.

"That is," added Neville, "if you dare to travel with me."

"I'll be glad to," said Warton, helping the mouse to his feet.

As Neville brushed himself off, Warton pointed upward. "Look! Now we know exactly which way to go!"

Neville cocked his head back. Far above him crows had begun to fill the afternoon sky. In twos and threes, alone and in groups, they drifted by. All were going in the same direction.

"They're flying toward Flat Mountain," said Neville.

"Then that's where we must go," said Warton.

Immediately, the toad and the mouse started out for Flat Mountain. After they had left the sandbank far behind, they entered a grove of white birches. It was when they were deep in the grove that Warton noticed the light was beginning to fade.

"We'll have to stop for the night soon," he said.

"I see just the place," said Neville. They were standing on a small rise, not far from a stream. "There's a tree that's fallen over the stream. We can sleep under its upturned roots, and in the morning we can use the tree to cross the stream."

"A perfect place," agreed Warton.

The toad and the mouse hurried on and were nearly to the tree when Warton stopped short. "Oh-oh. Someone has gotten here first."

Warton and Neville stared at tiny wisps of blue smoke that rose from behind the tree.

"I wonder if whoever has built that fire is friendly," said Neville.

"We'd better be careful, just in case," said Warton.

Stealthily, they approached the fallen tree. When they were close enough to hear the crackling of the fire, they stopped.

Then Warton saw something bright orange moving behind the tree. Then he saw a flash of something purple. Then he saw something brilliant green. Then he gasped.

"What is it?" asked Neville. "Is it horrible?"

Before Warton could answer, someone stepped from behind the tree.

"Grampa Arbuckle!" cried Warton. "It's you!"

"Well, of course it is," said the old toad, who was dressed in an orange jacket, purple pants, and green rubber boots. "Don't you recognize me in my exploring clothes?"

"I do," said Warton. "But I'm surprised to see you here."

"Well, you shouldn't be," grumbled the old toad. "Just because I'm old, that doesn't mean I should let some rude crow fly off with my most prized possession, does it?"

Warton shook his head.

Grampa Arbuckle turned to Neville. "And having a little rheumatism is no reason for not going after my watch-compass, is it?"

Neville shook his head.

"Of course it isn't," said Grampa Arbuckle. Then a twinkle appeared in his eyes. "And since you two are most likely here for the same reason as I, I think I should catch a few more minnows for supper than I was planning on."

"Oh, I have my own supper," said Warton.

"In that case," said Grampa Arbuckle, picking up his fishing pole, "I'll catch just enough for Neville and me."

"I'll come along to help," said Neville.

As Neville followed Grampa Arbuckle to the stream, Warton gathered more wood for the fire. After that, he rolled a log close to the flames for everyone to sit on. He was just about to try it out when a yell came from the stream.

Quickly Warton rushed to the stream. There he found his grandfather sitting at the water's edge with a very pained expression on his face. Neville was beside him.

"What happened?" asked Warton.

"Oh, Warton," said Neville, "it's all my fault. I was standing beside Grampa Arbuckle as he fished from a rock. When I bent over to tie my shoelace, I accidentally bumped him into the stream. Then, after he swam ashore and was drying out his boots, he stepped on some fishhooks I had spilled on the sand. That's when he yelled."

Neville looked at Warton with tears in his eyes.

31

"Nothing I do ever turns out right." He turned around and, with his rope tail dragging, went off toward the fire.

It took a while for Grampa Arbuckle to remove the last fishhook from his feet. When he was done, Warton helped him hobble back to the fallen tree. There Neville was sitting on the log before the fire, looking very dejected.

"Since there were no minnows caught," said Warton, "we can all eat some of Morton's delicious sandwiches." He opened his pack and passed the sandwiches around.

They ate quickly and silently. When they were done, Grampa Arbuckle yawned and said, "We've a high mountain to climb tomorrow, so I'm going to bed early." He said good night and lay down.

Warton turned to the mouse, who seemed deep in thought. "Will you help me get water from the stream so we can put out the fire?"

The mouse looked at Warton. "No," he said.

Warton could hardly believe what he had heard.

"I'm sorry, Warton," said the mouse. "But if I help you, I'll only cause an accident. You could drown or something." Then he took a deep breath. "I've decided that the best thing for me to do is . . . nothing. From now on, I'm never going to help anyone again." With that, the mouse lay down. "Good night, Warton."

As Warton fetched the water himself, he thought about Neville. "Perhaps he will change his mind in the morning," he thought as he poured water on the smoldering coals. Then he too went to sleep.

In the morning, when Warton awoke, a very pleasant aroma met his nose. He sat up and looked at the campfire, where Grampa Arbuckle was happily frying freshly caught minnows.

"I arose early and did a bit of fishing," said the old toad as Warton and Neville joined him. "I was lucky, as you can see." He turned to Neville. "Will you pass these tasty morsels around?"

"No," said Neville.

Grampa Arbuckle looked startled.

Warton whispered to his grandfather, "Neville's afraid he'll only cause more accidents if he helps."

"Oh," grunted Grampa Arbuckle. "Well, that makes sense."

Warton hoped Neville had not heard.

As soon as they had eaten breakfast, the toads and

the mouse were on their way. They crossed the stream, and after a while came to the bottom of Flat Mountain. Before them lay a steep zigzaggy path that was crisscrossed with rain ditches and cluttered with stones.

"It looks like it goes straight to the sky," said Warton.

With Grampa Arbuckle in front, Warton in the middle, and Neville last, they started up the mountain. As they climbed, the earth grew hot beneath their feet. There was not a breath of air to cool them off. They climbed the rest of that morning and through the noon hour. Then it was early afternoon, and that became late afternoon.

It was at that time that Grampa Arbuckle pointed to the sky. "Look," he said. "The crows are returning to their roosting place."

At first there was only one crow, but soon there were others. They came from all directions, and before long they filled the sky. Some sailed directly over the climbers' heads. Every bird was headed for the same place—somewhere beyond the top of the mountain.

They continued to climb. Higher and higher they went, until it seemed they would soon meet the red setting sun.

Then, as sand and stone and scrubby trees took on the pink colors of twilight, Warton, Grampa Arbuckle, and Neville pulled themselves over a clump of crusty earth and at last stood on top of Flat Mountain.

F lat Mountain was indeed flat. Its top was a land of brown grass and straggly bushes. Nothing else grew there except a ring of trees some distance away.

The first thing Warton saw was a few crows scattered about in the grass. Then, when he looked toward the ring of trees, he gasped. The tall trees were completely filled with crows. Every branch drooped under the weight of the large black birds, and the very air about the trees was alive with them.

"I've never seen so many crows at one time," said Neville.

"How will we ever find the one who took the watch-compass?" asked Warton.

"There's only one way," said Grampa Arbuckle. "Someone must go in there and speak to them. And that someone should be me."

"But *I* washed the watch-compass," said Neville. "I should go."

"And if *I* had returned it the night we played dominoes," said Warton, "it would not have gotten washed. I should go."

The toads and the mouse looked at one another.

Without another word the three started for the trees. As they went along, Warton was surprised to see a great number of small turtle shells lying all about the grassy field.

Then they came to the ring of trees. Warton felt uneasy as they entered the shadowy place, and when he looked up he thought every crow in the world had come to Flat Mountain. The din made by the chattering birds was so incredible, it was impossible to hear one another speak. Grampa Arbuckle pointed to a small clearing, and they all hurried toward it.

The clearing was set in the middle of the trees like a hole in a doughnut. When the toads and the mouse reached it they saw a most unusual sight. Standing in the clearing were four crows, each one sleek and strong. In the grass around the four crows and in the branches of the trees that ringed the clearing were hundreds and hundreds of trinkets, baubles, and gadgets. Under the last light of day, their glittering and sparkling gave the whole clearing an eerie glow.

With wide eyes Warton looked about. He saw buckles and buttons, pieces of metal and glass, bracelets and keys, thumbtacks and shoehorns, fountain pens and rings. "So this is where crows bring the things they take," he said.

"And somewhere here is my watch-compass," said Grampa Arbuckle. He went straight up to the largest crow in the clearing. "Harumph!" he said. "I have a question for you."

The big bird cocked his head and peered down at Grampa Arbuckle. "Do you realize to whom you are speaking?" he said disdainfully.

"Of course I don't," grumbled Grampa Arbuckle.

"Well, *I* happen to be Woobit, leader of all crows of the North. And these three are Moc, leader of the East, Sogglue, leader of the South, and Zoof, leader of the West. Now, what sort of business would two toads and a mouse have with us?"

"We're looking for the crow who flew off with my watch-compass," said Grampa Arbuckle.

"Why?" said Woobit of the North in a raspy voice.

"Because I want it back," said Grampa Arbuckle.

"That's too bad," said the crow. "Because you can't have it."

Grampa Arbuckle stiffened. "But it doesn't belong to that crow," he said.

"True," said the crow. "It belongs to no crow, yet it belongs to all crows."

Warton, Grampa Arbuckle, and Neville looked confused.

"I can see you don't understand the way of crows," said Woobit of the North. "I'll explain. Each autumn all crows from every part of the forest gather here for the winter. Every day we fly off to different places to feed. If someone sees something bright and pretty, he brings it back, and then it belongs to *all* crows to enjoy during the dark winter days . . . until the contests."

"Contests?" said Warton.

"Yes," said Woobit of the North. "When winter is gone, on the last day of our stay here, any crow may choose any object he would like to take with him for the summer. If more than one crow want the same thing, we have contests to decide who gets it. All day long there are several dozen contests going on at the same time."

"What kind of contests are they?" asked Neville.

"The most exciting kind there is," said Zoof of the West. "Turtle-shell-diving contests."

"That's when the crows who want the same thing fly high in the air," said Sogglue of the South. "Then a small turtle shell is dropped, and the one who catches it is the winner. But it's not easy to do, because turtle shells take sudden turns and go in all directions."

"But I can't enter a flying contest," said Grampa Arbuckle.

Moc of the East laughed. "Even if you could fly, you could not enter the contest. These contests are for crows only. So there is no way you can get your . . . your . . . whatever it is."

"It's called a watch-compass," said Grampa Arbuckle angrily. "Don't any of you even know what that is?"

The four crows shook their heads.

At that moment Warton spied a watch lying in the grass. He picked it up. "It looks like this, but it's a compass too, and not nearly so tarnished."

"Tarnished?" said Zoof of the West.

"Yes," said Warton. He rubbed the watch on his shirt-sleeve until it was bright. "See, this is the way

Grampa Arbuckle's watch-compass looks, though his is much brighter because he uses puffball powder and morning dew to polish it."

After Warton put the watch down, the crows gathered around it and began talking to one another in hushed tones.

"Well, now we know," said Grampa Arbuckle. "Crows are dumb, all right. They don't even know about polishing things."

"What should we do now?" said Neville.

"We can do nothing but go home, I'm afraid," said Grampa Arbuckle.

The two toads and the mouse turned about and started off.

"Stop!" came the raspy voice of Woobit of the North. "Where do you think you are going?"

"We're going home," replied Grampa Arbuckle.

The four crows hopped forward and quickly surrounded them.

"You aren't going anywhere!" said Moc of the East.

"What do you mean?" said Grampa Arbuckle.

"You are going to stay here a while," said the crow.

"But why?" said Warton. "For what purpose?"

Moc peered at Warton with a dark eye. "Why, haven't you guessed? For polishing purposes, of course. Now that we know how much prettier polishing can make things, we want *all* our things polished. And since our talons are too awkward for that work, we want you to do it for us."

"For the next two days," said Zoof of the West, "you are to polish all our things so they will look nice for the contests."

Before the stunned toads and the mouse could reply, Moc gave a loud caw and three husky crows flew out of the trees.

"Take them and guard them!" ordered the crow leader.

The three guard crows grabbed Grampa Arbuckle, Warton, and Neville and rose into the air. They flew over the ring of trees and landed beside a hollow log that lay in the field of brown grass.

"Get in there!" ordered one of the guard crows.

The toads and the mouse stepped inside the log and sat down on a floor of crumbly wood.

"Those crows have some nerve," said Warton. "Besides taking things that aren't theirs, they want others to do their work."

"Hmmmph!" grunted Grampa Arbuckle. "What do you expect from creatures with names like Woobit and Sogglue?"

"I'm glad it's only for two days," said Neville.

"Me too," said Warton. Then he opened his pack and passed around the last of Morton's sandwiches.

When they were finished eating, Warton leaned back against the rotty log. Grampa Arbuckle took off his spectacles and stretched out, and Neville curled up in a ball. Night settled upon Flat Mountain, and the tired captives went to sleep.

Next morning, Warton awoke to a sharp tapping sound. He hoped he'd been dreaming, and that Morton was tapping a spoon against his bed because he'd overslept. When he opened his eyes, he saw that he was in a hollow log, and that a crow was peering in at him.

"Come out here!" ordered the crow.

As soon as the toads and the mouse stepped outside, the guard crows grabbed them and flew off to the little clearing inside the ring of trees.

As Warton looked about, he had to squint. Under the bright morning sun the objects in the grass and in the trees were alive with dancing lights. It took him a while to become accustomed to the brightness. Then he noticed how quiet it was. "All the crows are gone!" he said.

"Of course they are," snapped one of the guard crows. "And when they return tonight they will expect the pretty things to be even prettier. Now get busy!"

The crow picked up a bag and emptied out a pile of puffballs. "We gathered these this morning while you slept."

Warton, Grampa Arbuckle, and Neville each broke

open the thin brittle covering of a puffball. They mixed some of the fine yellow powder with morning dew and started polishing.

All morning long they polished. They polished belt buckles and teaspoons, needles and pins, hinges and paper clips. They polished and they polished, and when they looked around at noontime there seemed to be just as much to do as before.

"We'll never polish everything in two days," said Warton.

"It's an impossible task," said Neville.

Grampa Arbuckle just grunted.

Toward the end of the afternoon, crows began drifting in to the ring of trees.

"That will be enough," said one of the guard crows.

Warton, Neville, and Grampa Arbuckle found themselves being whisked into the air again, and again they were set down by the hollow log in the field.

"Get inside," ordered one of the guards. "And get plenty of sleep so you can polish even better tomorrow."

"What about supper?" said Warton.

"Supper?" said the crow.

"Of course," said Grampa Arbuckle. "Don't you think we eat?"

The crow appeared perplexed. "I must speak to our leaders," he said and flew off.

In a few moments the guard crow was back. This time Woobit, leader of the North, was with him, and he carried a sack.

"Here is your supper," said Woobit. "And I promise we will not forget to feed you again . . . ever."

There was something about the way Woobit said "ever" that made Warton take notice. "What do you mean?" he asked.

"Well," replied the crow, "it appears you won't be able to polish all our things before the contests."

"It would take all summer," grumbled Grampa Arbuckle.

"Quite true," said the crow. "And then it will be winter, and more things will have arrived here. It's truly an endless job."

Warton feared what the crow would say next.

"So," said Woobit of the North, "we have decided that you three must stay here forever."

The toads and the mouse gasped.

"It won't be so bad," said the crow. "You will polish all day, and in return we will feed you and let you live in this nice log." He stretched his wings. "Eat and eat well." Then he flew off.

Warton and the others stared, speechless, after him.

"Get inside!" ordered a guard.

Warton picked up the bag, and the three went into the log. They sat, weary and dejected, on the rotted floor.

"We're to become slaves," said Neville.

"For polishing purposes," said Grampa Arbuckle.

"For the rest of our lives," said Warton.

Slowly, Grampa Arbuckle opened the sack. "And look at this," he grunted, "willow buds and dried millet seeds. Some fare for the rest of our lives—bird food!"

For a while the three prisoners sat quietly. Then

Warton looked at Grampa Arbuckle, Grampa Arbuckle looked at Neville, Neville looked at Warton, and together they whispered, "We must escape!"

"But how?" asked Warton.

"I don't know," said Grampa Arbuckle.

"Me neither," said Neville.

They were silent again.

Then Grampa Arbuckle said, "I wonder if crows see well in the dark."

"I've never seen one fly at night," said Neville.

"Then perhaps that's when we can escape," said Warton.

"And the sooner we try, the better," said Grampa Arbuckle.

"I agree," said Neville. "I've done enough polishing."

"Let's go tonight," said Warton.

"Let's," said Grampa Arbuckle. "We'll wait until it's very late, then we'll sneak away."

Warton and Neville nodded.

After the toads and the mouse ate as much bird food as they could, they took turns napping as they awaited the late hours of the night.

Warton and Neville were fast asleep when Grampa Arbuckle shook them. "Wake up!" whispered the old toad. "One of the guards has fallen asleep, and the other two are so busy telling stories, they aren't paying any attention to us at all."

Quickly, Warton and Neville got to their feet. Then all three peeked out one end of the log. They saw the sleeping crow, and beyond him the other two crows busily telling stories. They went to the other end of the log. After waiting a few moments, they cautiously stepped out under the star-filled sky. On their tiptoes, they started out across the field of brown grass.

Almost at once a loud caw pierced the night air.

Warton's heart leaped into his throat. "Oh, no!" he cried. "They've seen us!"

"But we decided crows can't see at night," said Neville.

"It looks as though we were very, very wrong about that," said Grampa Arbuckle. "Run for your lives!"

Warton ran as he had never run before. He heard more caws go up, and then more. Soon the sound of thousands of crows cawing at once was coming toward him. The voices of the angry birds grew louder and

52

louder, and the sound reverberated over his head in waves. He looked up and with horror saw the night sky so filled with flying crows that he could no longer see the stars. With the sound of a multitude of beating wings falling upon him like rain, Warton turned his attention back to the ground. To his dismay, Grampa Arbuckle and Neville were nowhere to be seen.

Then, from somewhere in the grass, he heard a familiar voice.

"Put me down, you dumb bird! Go do your own polishing!"

Warton's heart quickened. "That's Grampa Arbuckle!"

From a different direction he heard another voice.

"Hey, stop that! Let go of my tail!"

"Oh no!" thought Warton. "Now they have Neville!"

Warton wanted to go to them, but he knew that wouldn't help anyone. So he did the only thing he could. He ran and ran and ran.

He expected dark wings to settle over him at any moment and snatch him up too. But, somehow, no crow discovered him. To his surprise he soon found himself at the very edge of Flat Mountain. He leaped over the side and tumbled downward until he rolled against two flat rocks that made a sort of cave.

Warton crouched under the rocks, listening to the crows cawing overhead. After a long time the birds flew off.

"Now," said Warton, "I must think of a way to help Grampa Arbuckle and Neville get away." He said it over and over until he drifted into an uneasy sleep.

Warton had several dreams. He dreamed of Grampa Arbuckle and Neville polishing for the rest of their lives. He dreamed of hordes of crows filling a night sky. He dreamed of a gold watch-compass, and he dreamed of a blind blue jay sitting in a walnut tree.

Suddenly he sat up, wide awake. As he stared into the darkness, his eyes began blinking. It was something he always did when he thought very hard. For a while he blinked furiously, then he stopped. "That's it!" he cried. He hopped up and stepped out from under the rock, and he saw that all was still dark.

"If my plan is to work," he said, "I can't wait till morning." With determined steps he set out on a night journey.

Warton's journey took him back to the bottom of Flat Mountain, and then to the little stream in the grove of white birches. By that time, the darkness was gone and the soft blue light of early morning had taken its place. Warton paused by what had once been the campfire he had sat beside only a few nights before. "Good," he said. "There's plenty for what I'll need."

He continued on his way. After he struggled through the thick laurel bushes, he saw the lone walnut tree in the center of the small meadow. He heard the crash of a rock hitting another rock. "Sounds like Bike is eating breakfast," he said to himself.

He hurried to the tree and found the blue jay pulling a piece of walnut from its shell. "Bike!" he cried. "It's me, Warton!"

Bike's head snapped up. "Warton, what are you doing here?"

"My grandfather and a mouse friend are in serious trouble," replied Warton. He then explained what the crows had done.

"That's terrible," said Bike. "But why did you come here?"

"You can help," said Warton. "But the plan I have is dangerous, and I'll understand if you don't want to do it."

Bike looked surprised. "Warton, don't you know that to someone who sits in a tree all day eating walnuts, a little danger sounds wonderful? Now, tell me your plan."

"Well," said Warton, "when I remembered your big pack and how strong you are, it occurred to me that you might be able to fly in among the crows with me in the pack to guide you. Then, when the guards aren't watching, Grampa Arbuckle and Neville can sneak into the pack with me, and we'll fly away."

"I could do that easily," said Bike. "But you've forgotten one thing. A blue jay among crows is sure to be noticed."

"Oh, I have a plan for that, too," said Warton. "We'll disguise you to look like a crow."

The blue jay looked astonished. "Disguise me?"

"Yes," said Warton. "I'm quite sure it would work."

"A disguise?" said Bike again. "Fly in among thousands of nasty crows? Carry two toads and a mouse in a pack? Warton, that sounds like it could be very, very exciting. Let's go!"

The blue jay flew up into a hole in the tree. When he appeared again, he had on a large red pack. He landed beside Warton and said, "There are scissors inside for making eyeholes."

Warton climbed into the spacious pack and cut out several small holes. When he was done, the blue jay took to the air. First they had to devise a way for Warton to tell Bike which way to go. They found that taps worked best. A tap to one side and Bike went one way, a tap to the other side and he went the other way. Two taps meant go up, and three meant go down. Soon Bike was flying as well as any sighted bird, and he passed swiftly over the forest trees.

When the grove of white birches came into sight, Warton signaled Bike to land beside the old campfire.

"Now," said the toad, "it's time for your disguise."

Warton picked up some charcoal and began rubbing it into the bird's feathers. In a short while the blue jay was no longer blue. Instead, from head to tail, he was a deep, rich black.

Warton stepped back to admire his work. "Oh-oh," he said.

"What's wrong?" asked Bike.

"I forgot your crest," said Warton. "Crows don't have any."

The blue jay sighed. "Oh well, I can always grow another one. Cut it off, Warton."

Warton snipped off the crest feathers, and again he stepped back to look. "Bike," he said, "you make a fine crow."

"Thank you," said the blue jay.

Warton hopped back into the pack, and the disguised blue jay rose up and sailed off. Bike flew even faster than before, and before Warton knew it, they were flying over the rim of Flat Mountain.

"The contests must have already started," said Warton, seeing many small groups of crows flying all about the field of brown grass.

"Describe them to me," said Bike.

"Well," said Warton as they flew along, "it appears the crows who are interested in a certain object first place it in the grass. Then they go high in the air to dive after a small turtle shell when it's dropped. Whoever catches it gets the pretty object."

"And what are those strange sounds I hear?" asked Bike.

Warton listened. Then he heard a hollow whistling. "That must be all those turtle shells falling through the air."

"Oh," said Bike. "I'll bet it's fun."

They now had come to the ring of trees, and Warton saw the small clearing. Unlike the first time he had seen it, when only the four crow leaders were there, many crows were now present. Each was trying

60

to decide which pretty thing to take to his summer
home.

Warton directed Bike to fly slowly around the clear-
ing as he searched for Grampa Arbuckle and Neville.
With each passing moment he became more worried.
Then he cried out, "There they are!"

Sitting in a patch of dirt, the old toad and the
mouse were busy polishing. Warton noticed that
Grampa Arbuckle's spectacles were broken, and half of
Neville's rope tail was missing. He wished he could go
straight to them, but this was not the time. He directed Bike to land some distance from them.

"We'll have to wait a while," said Warton, "till I think of a way to tell Grampa Arbuckle and Neville that we are here."

"Okay," said Bike. "I'll pretend I'm a crow in the meantime."

As Warton studied the situation, Bike began to strut in a crowlike manner. He cocked his head as if he were looking at the things in the grass. Now and then he made strange-sounding caws.

While Bike was strutting about, Warton noticed that the guard crows did not once take their eyes off Grampa Arbuckle and Neville. "This is not going to be easy," he thought. Suddenly Warton felt a hard bump that knocked him on his back. At once he realized he had forgotten all about directing Bike.

"Oh, excuse me," he heard Bike say. "I'm afraid I didn't see you there."

"Well, be more careful," said a crow.

"I will," said Bike. "I certainly will."

As Warton struggled to get back to the eyehole, he heard the crow speak again. "Say, you're quite small for a crow, aren't you?"

Warton gulped.

"I've been sick," answered Bike without hesitating. "In fact, this is the first year I've been well enough to come here. Thanks to all the medicine I carry in my pack."

"I see," said the crow. "And what's your name?"

"Bike," replied the blue jay. "What's yours?"

"Woobit, leader of the North," said the crow.

"Oh no!" groaned Warton. He squirmed around until at last he was able to look out the eyehole. With a gasp he saw the four crow leaders staring at Bike.

Woobit spoke again. "There's something strange about you, Bike. Which part of the forest are you from? It's certainly not my part, the North."

"And it's not my part, the South," said Sogglue.

"Nor mine, the East," said Moc.

"And if you aren't from my part, the West, which you aren't," said Zoof, "then which part of the forest *are* you from?"

Warton's heart was racing.

"Which part of the forest am I from?" said Bike. "Why, I'm from . . . I'm from . . . Center Forest!"

"Center Forest?" said all four crow leaders.

"Yes," said Bike. "Everything has a center, hasn't it?"

64

"Of course," said Zoof.

"Well, the forest has one too," said Bike. "And that's where I'm from."

"Is that so," said Moc. "Then tell me why I've never met any other crows from there."

Bike was silent a while. Then he said, "You haven't seen other crows from there because, being Center Forest—the very exact center—it's a very tiny spot, as all exact centers are. It's so small, in fact, that there's room for only one crow there . . . me—leader of Center Forest!"

Warton held his breath.

"Hmmm," said Sogglue. "That sounds reasonable."

"It does," said Woobit. "You definitely have a right to be here, Bike, so pick whatever you want from within the ring of trees."

"Pick whatever I want?" said Bike.

"Of course," said Sogglue. "Don't you know the rules—that all winter long everything here belongs to all crows, but on this last day a crow may claim anything for his very own?"

"Oh," said Bike. "Well, of course I know *that*."

"Then choose something," said Moc.

Inside the pack Warton was feeling extremely nervous. He knew that if the crows suspected Bike of being blind they would look in the pack immediately. "Yet," thought Warton, "how is a blind blue jay to pick out something he can't see?" He held his breath.

"Well?" said Woobit. "Don't you see something you like?"

"Certainly I do," said Bike slowly. "I'd like . . . I'd like . . . those polishers—the old toad and the mouse!"

Warton gasped.

"The two polishers!" exclaimed the four crows at once.

"Yes," said Bike. "Didn't you say anything within the trees?"

"Well, yes," said Sogglue.

"Good," said Bike. "That's what I want."

The four crows looked at each other.

"Well, I'm certainly not going to let this pip-squeak have them," said Woobit. "I claim them for the crows of the North!"

"Then I claim them for the crows of the South!" said Sogglue.

"I claim them also!" said Moc and Zoof.

"Then it's to be a contest of leaders!" declared Woobit.

"Off to the contest field!" cried Zoof.

Grampa Arbuckle and Neville were whisked away by the guards. All the other crows followed after the four leaders, and there was no one left but Bike and his secret passenger.

Looking stunned, Warton poked his head out of the pack. He could see by Bike's expression that the blue jay was as surprised as he by the sudden turn of events.

"Warton," said Bike, "when I had to choose something, your grandfather and mouse friend were all I was certain of."

"You did the only thing possible," said Warton. "The trouble is, now things have gotten much worse. Grampa Arbuckle and Neville are to be prizes in a contest the four most powerful crows of all will be trying to win, and there is nothing we can do about it."

Bike bobbed his head up and down. "Things have gotten worse, all right," he said. "But there *is* something we can do about it."

Warton looked perplexed. "What do you mean?"

"Why, what else?" said Bike. "I'll just have to enter that contest and catch the turtle shell myself."

Warton gasped. "You? Catch the turtle shell?"

"Why not?" said Bike. "You heard the sound they make as they fall. Well, I'm quite good at catching things that make a bit of sound. And with you to guide me, I think we can do it."

For several moments Warton was speechless. Then in a determined voice he said, "All right, Bike, let's go enter that contest!"

As soon as Warton sat back down inside the pack, the blue jay rose into the air and headed for the contest field.

Flying over the ring of trees, Warton saw that the field of brown grass had become a sea of black birds. Every crow was there to watch the contest between the leaders. In the center of all the birds was a tiny open space. There Warton saw the hollow log where he had once been kept prisoner. Now Grampa Arbuckle and Neville were tied to it by long ropes, to keep them from running off during the excitement of the contest. Nearby stood the four crow leaders.

Warton directed Bike to a landing in the small open space.

"Who's that?" asked one crow.

"I hear he's from Center Forest," answered another crow.

"And is he the leader?" asked the first crow.

"He must be," said the second crow. "He's the only one who lives there."

"Attention," called a crow with a yellow ribbon around his neck. "As dropper of the turtle shell I say it is time to start the contest." He picked up a turtle shell and rose into the air. A roar went up from the crowd as the contestants followed after him.

Inside the pack, Warton was troubled. "Is it possible," he wondered, "for a small blue jay to be any match for four powerful crows?"

In another moment came the sad answer. Looking up, he saw that the crows were already high above Bike.

Then one of the crows cawed.

"Warton," said Bike, "are the crows higher than I?"

Warton hardly had the heart to answer. "I'm afraid they are," he said.

"Then I must try harder," grunted Bike.

As Bike's wings beat furiously, Warton could feel their great power, and he knew it came from all the times Bike had lifted the heavy rock he used for opening walnuts. When Warton looked up again he was amazed to see that the crows were now close by.

"Bike," he said, "you're as high as the crows."

"Good," huffed the blue jay.

Seeing that the crows were soaring around in small

circles now, Warton directed Bike to do the same.

Then the turtle-shell dropper cawed. "Get ready to dive!" He began to count. "One . . ."

Warton felt Bike give a nervous shiver.

"Two . . ."

Warton took a deep breath.

"Three!" The turtle shell was dropped.

The four crows let out loud caws as they plunged after it. With wings folded back Bike, too, took pursuit. Inside the pack, Warton peered out. He felt wind rushing past him. He saw the earth coming toward him at incredible speed. His stomach seemed to rise up and float by itself, and he suddenly felt rather strange. But as uncomfortable as he felt, he dared not take his eyes off the turtle shell. He watched as it flipped, flopped, spun, and curved toward the ground. And he listened to the ghostly sounds it made as it passed through the air—the very sounds that told Bike exactly which way to go.

Then, as Bike began getting closer to the turtle shell, Warton saw that the crows were getting closer, too. The five birds were now so near each other their feathers touched. Then Moc bumped against Bike. That made Bike bump Sogglue.

"Watch where you're going!" snapped Sogglue. He flipped his tail against Bike so hard that the blue jay went into a triple somersault.

As Bike turned over and over, Warton saw the turtle shell getting smaller and smaller. "Bike!" he cried. "We're falling behind!"

Immediately, the blue jay gave several quick beats of his strong wings. The faster speed nearly blinded Warton, but soon they were once again in among the four crows.

The big birds were jostling one another fiercely as they chased the turtle shell. Woobit gave Zoof a shove that sent him tumbling through the air. Sogglue thumped a wing against Moc's belly, and he went fluttering away.

Warton was glad to see at least two crows out of the way. But then he saw that the turtle shell was now directly in front of Sogglue. Horrified, he watched as the crow opened his beak wide.

Warton could think of only one thing to do. He picked up the scissors, which were still in the pack, and he cut a hole in the bottom of the pack. Then he snipped off one of Bike's feathers. "I hope Bike doesn't mind," he thought.

Moving swiftly, Warton poked the feather through one of the eyeholes. He reached out until he was able to touch one of Sogglue's feet. Then he rubbed the feather back and forth, and just as the crow was about to snap up the turtle shell he began to giggle. Soon he was laughing so hard he could hardly see, and instead of biting the shell he bit Woobit. With a cry of pain Woobit went sailing away in one direction while Sogglue, laughing wildly, went another way.

All the time, the turtle shell was dropping. Now it was dangerously near the hard earth.

"Bike!" cried Warton. "There's not much time left!"

"Then hold on tight," said Bike. He opened his beak and snapped it shut on the turtle shell. The turtle shell kept falling.

"Oh no!" moaned Warton. "Bike's beak is too small to hold on to the shell!" His heart sank, and his head filled with thoughts of Grampa Arbuckle and Neville spending the rest of their lives polishing. He was completely surprised by what Bike did next.

The blue jay simply wrapped his wings around the turtle shell and, looking like a ball of feathers, dropped even faster. Warton was sure they would smash against the ground, but then, at the last moment, Bike opened his wings, and clutching the turtle shell firmly with his feet, he shot upward.

"Bike!" exclaimed Warton. "You did it! You won the contest!"

"I did, didn't I!" shouted the blue jay. He spread his wings and made three loops for joy. Then he landed in the field of grass.

At once, the four crow leaders gathered around him.

"I thought surely Woobit was going to catch the turtle shell," said Zoof.

"I would have," said Woobit, "if Sogglue hadn't bit me."

"I didn't do it on purpose," said Sogglue. "But for some strange reason I developed a tickle in my foot." Suddenly, he turned and stared at the blue jay. "Bike," he said slowly, "I knew you were a peculiar-looking crow when I first saw you. Now I know something else about you."

Inside the pack Warton swallowed hard.

"And that is," said Sogglue, "that you are the best flyer of any crow I've ever seen."

Warton let out a sigh of relief.

"That's right," said Zoof. "You could win any contest here."

"Really?" said Bike. "Well, perhaps I will enter another . . ."

Warton quickly gave Bike a hard poke.

"I mean, no thank you. I'll just take my polishers and go."

"Very well," said Moc. He called to two guard crows. "Bring the polishers here."

At once the guards untied the long ropes from the log, and with the ends in their beaks they led the old toad and the mouse over to where the crow leaders and Bike stood.

"They're all yours now," said Woobit. "I imagine you are eager to take them to your summer home, eh?"

"Oh, I'm going to take them home, all right," said Bike. Then in a gruff voice he said, "You two climb into my pack now, and be careful not to step on my special medicine in there!"

Slowly, Grampa Arbuckle, who still had the long rope trailing after him, climbed onto Bike's back. Angrily, he lifted the lid of the pack. When he saw Warton crouched down inside looking up at him, he caught his breath. Warton winked, and at once the old toad realized what was happening. Pretending to grumble, he quickly hopped into the pack.

Neville was next. He jumped onto Bike's back, he too with the long rope still attached.

Down in the pack, Warton could hardly wait to see the surprised look on Neville's face. Then the lid opened. Neville peered inside, and Warton did indeed see a surprised face. In fact, the little mouse was *so* surprised that he staggered backward and tumbled off Bike's back. With a thud he landed on the ground. Quickly he hopped up, but now he was a bit dazed, and in his confusion he started going away from Bike.

"Hey!" shouted one of the guards. "This one doesn't want to go!"

"Well, we'll see about that," said the other guard. He went over to Neville and swatted him to the ground with his wing.

Now Neville was even more confused. When he got up, he went in another wrong direction. This time the other guard swatted him.

Inside the pack, Warton could see it all, and he was so alarmed by the battering the mouse was taking that he jumped up. "I've got to get Neville in here at once—while there's still a chance of escape!"

"Wait for me," said Grampa Arbuckle. "If you plan on getting that mouse to do something right, you're going to need help."

Together, the toads climbed out of the pack. "Bike," said Warton, "be prepared to fly at a moment's notice."

"I'm ready," said Bike.

Warton and Grampa Arbuckle gave great leaps, and they landed at Neville's side.

"Hey, look!" shouted a guard. "Now there are two toads!"

"Where'd the other one come from?" said the second guard.

"Can't you see?" cried Zoof. "He's the toad that got away! Now he's returned to help his friends escape!"

"Then that bird must be helping them too," yelled Moc. "He's not a crow after all!"

"Stop them!" screeched the four crow leaders. "Stop them!"

But Warton and Grampa Arbuckle already had hold of Neville. They pushed him swiftly over to Bike's

side. There they helped the befuddled mouse onto Bike's back. Grampa Arbuckle jumped on. Then it was Warton's turn. He jumped. Just as he did, a guard crow fanned out a large wing, making a wall of black feathers. Warton hit against it and dropped to the ground.

As he lay there, he realized there was only one thing he could do now, and he did it. "Bike!" he cried out. "Fly! Fly away now!"

At once the blue jay took to the air. With his wings flapping furiously, he was off over the grassy field before any of the great hoard of crows understood what was happening. To them he was just a small crow flying off to his summer home.

Warton, who knew differently, hoped with all his heart that the blue jay, the mouse, and the old toad would make it to safety. A lump grew in his throat as he realized he would never see them again.

Then a guard picked Warton up with a scaly foot and roughly tossed him in the direction of the four crow leaders.

"Well, well," said Woobit. "It's the toad called Warton."

"He's the one who devised this escape plan," said Moc.

"He thought he could make fools of us!" said Sog-glue.

"We must make sure he never tries that again!" said Zoof.

The four crow leaders bobbed their heads up and down, and then, as one, they screeched, "Peck him to pieces!"

Slowly the four crows started toward the little toad.

Warton tried frantically to think of some way to stop them. He searched the grass about him. Seeing a silver ring he picked it up and, in desperation, threw it at Zoof. Zoof only laughed as it bounced off his slick feathers. Then Warton saw a small spoon. He threw that at Woobit. That, being a bit heavier, made a clunk sound as it hit Woobit on the head. But it didn't stop the crow, it only made him angrier. Warton searched about again, seeking something larger. Then he saw it. A golden object glistened in the noonday sun. Warton picked it up.

"Grampa Arbuckle's watch-compass! At last I've found it!" For a moment he looked at it closely. Then there was no time left. When he looked up, he saw eight dark eyes filled with hate, and four yellow beaks poised to strike. He heard low, throaty cawing sounds coming from each crow.

Then Warton heard something else. Somewhere, someone was calling his name. "Warton!" It seemed to come from above. He looked up.

Not far off, a small bird was flying through the sky. Warton stared hard at the bird, as did everyone else, for the bird was not flying the way birds usually do. At times he would go straight up. Then he would go in a circle. Then he would dip downward, once skimming over the heads of some very startled crows. When he went up again he flew, unbelievably, upside-down.

Warton gasped. "It can't be . . . but it is . . . it's Bike!"

The voice came again. "Warton, we're coming for you!"

Warton was astounded. "That voice . . . it's . . . it's Neville!"

By now, the disguised blue jay was high in the sky and going even higher. When he was directly over the

spot where Warton and the four leaders stood, his wings stopped flapping and the bird began falling. Faster and faster he went. Like a rock he plummeted down—straight toward the four crows and the toad.

"What's that crazy bird doing?" cried Woobit nervously.

"He's going to crash right here where we're standing, that's what!" yelled Moc.

"Then get out of my way!" shouted Sogglue. "I don't want to get killed!"

With that, all four crow leaders hopped quickly away.

Warton, his mouth agape, stood where he was. He watched as Bike came closer and closer to the ground. It was only a matter of moments before he would crash. Then Neville's voice was heard again.

"Better turn up now, Bike."

In an instant, the blue jay changed directions and swooped upward. He made a small circle, a head popped out of the pack, and a rope was dropped over Bike's side.

"Grab the rope and hold on tight!" called Neville.

Warton reached out. He took hold of the rope as it

swept past, and he found himself being whisked away over the heads of thousands of stunned crows. By the time anyone realized what had happened, Bike, with Neville inside the pack and Warton dangling from the rope, had disappeared over the rim of Flat Mountain.

Under Neville's direction, the blue jay flew down the mountainside. Then he went out over the treetops of the forest, and in a zigzaggy way headed for a particular tree—a huge dead elm that rose far above the other trees. As they came near the tree, something caught Warton's eye. On the very topmost branch he thought he saw a familiar figure. When he looked closer he knew who it was and he let out a cry.

"Grampa Arbuckle!"

The old toad was holding on for dear life with his eyes shut tightly. But when he heard Warton's cry, his eyes popped open. He seemed unable to believe what he saw as Warton, dangling from the end of the rope, passed directly before him. "Warton!" he cried. "Is that you?"

The sound of the old toad's voice was all Bike needed. He easily made a perfect landing on the little branch alongside Grampa Arbuckle. As soon as he did,

Warton climbed up the rope, and he and his grandfather gave each other big hugs.

"My boy!" exclaimed the old toad. "I'm so happy to see you're safe!" Then he peered down to the ground far, far below, and he began to shiver. "Now if I can only get back to earth, I'll be even happier."

"I'll take care of that right away," said Bike. "Hop on."

Grampa Arbuckle looked anxiously at Bike. "Who . . . who's going to guide you?"

Neville stuck his head out of the pack. "Perhaps Warton should," he said forlornly. "If *I* do, we may all get killed."

Grampa Arbuckle breathed a deep sigh of relief. Then he and Warton climbed onto Bike's back, and the blue jay quickly took his passengers down to the bottom of the big tree, and everyone moved into the cool shadows of some spreading ferns.

"My, my," said Grampa Arbuckle. "It certainly feels good to have dirt under my feet again."

"How did you get in that tree, anyway?" asked Warton.

"Well," said Grampa Arbuckle, "when you got caught by the crows and told Bike to fly off, he explained that someone would have to guide him because he was blind. I tried it first, but it seems I'm not meant to fly because I got deathly airsick at once."

"So I took over," said Neville sadly. "I meant to land in a clearing but somehow I caused Bike to land up in that tree."

"By then," said Grampa Arbuckle, "there was no

87

time to do anything except think of a way to save you from the crows before it was too late."

"And the only plan we could think of," said Bike, "was to fly right back there and, using the ropes that had been tied around your grandfather and Neville, see if we could rescue you somehow."

"Well, it worked out fine," said Warton. "And I'm as thankful as can be." Then he reached into his pocket and went over to Grampa Arbuckle. "I'm also thankful I happened to see this lying in the grass. Look."

The old toad gasped. "My watch-compass! You found it! What a wonderful surprise." His eyes glistened as he studied it. "I'd forgotten how beautiful it is. It's been some time since I've seen it, you know. Let's see . . . when was that exactly?"

"It was just before I came by," said Neville glumly. "That's when things started to happen to all of you."

There was a silence.

Then Bike turned toward the mouse. "You're something, Neville," he said.

Neville looked downcast. "I know," he said. "It's always been that way with me." He wiped a tear from his eye. "I'm sorry."

"Sorry?" said Bike. "For what? Because of you I've had more excitement in a short while than I've had before in my whole life. I can't thank you enough. Now when I'm sitting in my walnut tree, as bored as can be, I've got exciting memories to think of again and again."

Neville appeared perplexed. "You enjoyed all this?"

"I'm sorry to see it end," replied Bike.

For several moments Neville was lost in thought. "Say," he said finally. "You wouldn't care to have a mouse guide you all the time, would you? I mean, if you don't mind a few accidents, I'd be glad to direct you to any place in the forest you'd like."

Bike looked overjoyed. "That sounds like great fun," he said.

Grampa Arbuckle began to grunt. He looked down at his watch-compass, and he looked at Bike and Neville. Then, shaking his head, he went over to the mouse and the blue jay. "If you two are going to go traveling all over the forest, you're going to need all the help you can get. You'd better take this with you."

"But this is your watch-compass," said Neville.

"Of course it is," grumbled the old toad. "And if

you use it properly, you may not get lost too badly."

Gratefully, Neville took the watch-compass.

"Now I believe I'll start for home," said Grampa Arbuckle.

Everyone said good-bye.

Bike and Neville were the first to leave, and with anxious eyes Warton and Grampa Arbuckle watched as the mouse guided the blue jay. At first Bike went almost straight up. Then he went in a square. The two toads cringed as the blue jay flew directly toward an oak tree. At the last moment, the bird turned, made a sort of figure five, and amid a few fluttering oak leaves disappeared over the forest.

For a while the two toads trudged along silently. Then Warton said, "I was certainly surprised when you gave them your most prized possession. That was very nice of you."

"Hmmmph!" grunted the old toad. "It wasn't so nice of me." A twinkle came into his eyes, and he looked at Warton fondly. "Perhaps that wasn't my most prized possession after all."

The toads continued on toward their homes.